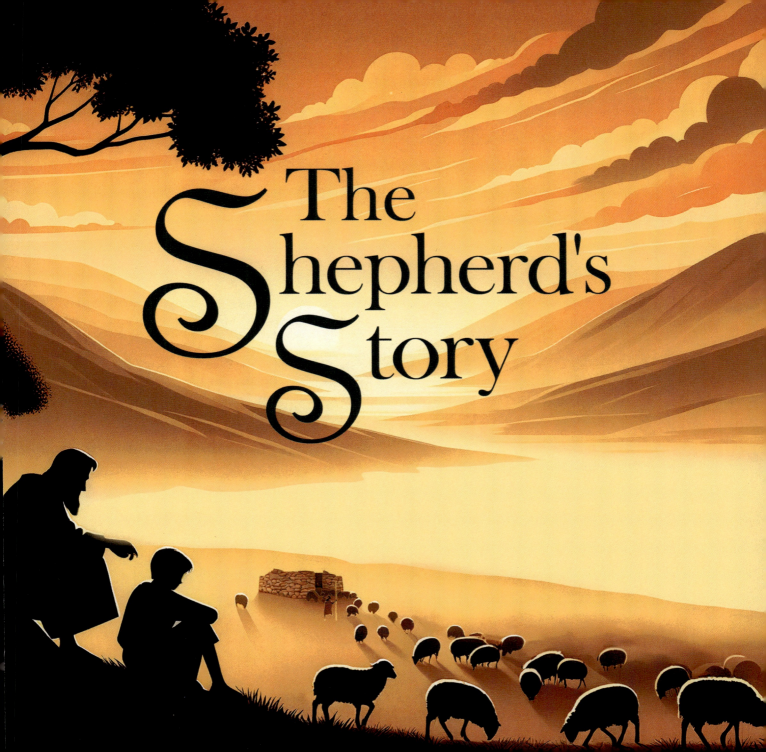

The Shepherd's Story

WestBow Press books may be ordered through booksellers or by contacting:

WestBow Press
A Division of Thomas Nelson & Zondervan
1663 Liberty Drive
Bloomington, IN 47403
www.westbowpress.com
844-714-3454

Because of the dynamic nature of the Internet, any web addresses or links contained in this book may have changed since publication and may no longer be valid. The views expressed in this work are solely those of the author and do not necessarily reflect the views of the publisher, and the publisher hereby disclaims any responsibility for them.

Any people depicted in stock imagery provided by Getty Images are models, and such images are being used for illustrative purposes only.
Certain stock imagery © Getty Images.

Scripture quotations are from the ESV® Bible (The Holy Bible, English Standard Version®), copyright © 2001 by Crossway, a publishing ministry of Good News Publishers. Used by permission. All rights reserved.

Scripture quotations taken from the (NASB®) New American Standard Bible®, Copyright © 1960, 1971, 1977, 1995, 2020 by The Lockman Foundation. Used by permission. All rights reserved. www.lockman.org

ISBN: 979-8-3850-2307-3 (sc)
979-8-3850-2309-7 (hc)
979-8-3850-2308-0 (e)

Library of Congress Control Number: 2024908548

Print information available on the last page.

WestBow Press rev. date: 04/29/2024

WESTBOW
PRESS®
A DIVISION OF THOMAS NELSON
& ZONDERVAN

The Shepherd's Story

By **Barbara Velure**

Illustrated by **David Davis** and **Margie Wall**

It was a clear, quiet, star-filled night sky as father and son were sitting on a hill overlooking the field where their sheep were bedded down for the night.

Tell me again, father, about that night when you were my age – that night which you said started out just like this one.

Now that's a story I never tire of the telling, son.

Clearing his throat, his father began to relate again the extraordinary events of that night a generation ago.

Like you remembered, son, it was a night so much like this one that I tremble to think about it. I was just your age. Our family was tending our sheep in this very same field.

It was a chilly night, but the stars were so bright that you felt you could reach out and grab one or two.

At that the father reached over and tickled his son, who giggled at the thought.

It was quiet like tonight. All you could hear were sheep now and then softly bleating their contentment.

I often gaze out on a night like this and think of the song that David wrote so long ago:

> **When I look at your heavens,**
> **the work of your fingers,**
> **the moon and the stars,**
> **which you have set in place,**
> **what is man that you are mindful of him,**
> **the son of man that you care for him?** [1]

The father paused to reflect upon the deep meaning of those words, humming softly to himself, lost in thought.

Then he felt a little nudge (not quite a tickle) from his son.

Go on. Tell me the rest of the story.

It was then that all of a sudden, the sky lit up and we saw what I guess was an angel (though I had never seen one before). He was surrounded with light which I imagine was like the glory that filled the temple when Solomon dedicated it.

You remember me telling you about that time, don't you?

Yes, father.

The light was so bright it was hard to see – it really took our breath away.

We were all so terribly frightened, wondering what would cause this to happen.

What had we done?

What was the reason for this?

But the angel spoke! interjected the son.

Yes!
I heard him say quite clearly Don't be afraid!
which was very hard to do!
But then he said he was bringing us good news –
joyful news – for everyone, not just to us there in the field.
He said that a baby was born that very day in the town of David.

And he meant Bethlehem, didn't he father! exclaimed the son.

Yes he did! nodded the father.
Because that's where David was born, too!
And then he said the baby was to be the Messiah!

Do you know why I thought it might be true?
The father looked intently at his son.

Yes, father.
The Scriptures say that the Messiah was going to be from there
because he was to be a descendant of King David.

That's right! answered the father.

But that wasn't all!
*He gave us a sign - **just for us**!*

Just for us? gaped the son, wide-eyed.

I think so, said the father excitedly, *because he said we would find the baby wrapped in strips of cloth and lying in a manger.*

In strips of cloth?
Lying in a manger?
gasped the son.

Yes!
Just like we take care of the newborn lambs that will eventually be taken for sacrifice at the temple in Jerusalem.

So you knew where to look! The son exclaimed, jumping up and down.

Yes! In one of the caves where our sheep have their lambs! Just think! The Messiah born like one of the little lambs! Not in a grand house where we couldn't go – since we're considered "unclean".

Wow! And you went, too! pumped the son, dancing around as if to go himself.

We sure did! as the father motioned the son to sit again. *But even before we could get up and go, there was suddenly* an army of angels praising God.

Awed, the son whispered, *And you understood what they were saying?*

We did! They said

> *Glory to God in the highest.*
> *Peace on earth to men*
> *with whom He is pleased.*[2]

Did they really say that God was pleased with men?!
pondered the son.
What did men do to please God?!!

Nothing, my son.
Only those who have faith in God please him.
But God was pleased to send the Messiah so that men could
be redeemed back into his good grace.

Oh. paused the son......*Then what happened?!*

Well, the angels went back to heaven, I guess, because we didn't see them anymore. And we just sat there in amazement catching our breath and staring at where they had been.

The father was still lost in thought reminiscing and reliving that magnificent spectacle.

Father? whispered the son.
Father! shaking his father's arm.

Sorry, son. I was lost in the wonder of it all.
.....Now, where were we?

The angels had left, the son responded.

Oh, yes! Well, we didn't sit staring very long! We all agreed that there was something to see and off we went.

Seeing the look of consternation on his son's face and knowing what he was thinking, he assured him that the sheep were left in his cousin Jacob's care.
Continuing, he told how they found the baby and his parents.

And the baby was lying in a manger wrapped in cloths! The son remembered.

Yes! Exactly like the angel had told us.

Did he look different? – I mean, the angel said he was the Messiah.

No, he looked just like any other baby boy.
The mother was very young and … radiant.

I don't remember if we said anything or they if they did, but
we sure did tell A LOT of people when we left!
And some remembered what the prophets had said and believed
that we had seen the Messiah! Though some couldn't figure
*out why **we** got to see him and why he was bedded in a manger;*
they thought he would be born at least more respectably like
his ancestor David's sons.

Curious, the son asked, *Why do you think he was born in a*
cave like our lambs?

The only thing I can figure is that they may have come for
the census that Caesar required and couldn't find any other
place to stay, pondered the father.

I sure hope they didn't stay there too long! he continued. *You remember me telling you about King Herod's decree not long after that to kill all the baby boys in Bethlehem.*

Yes! And I'm glad I wasn't born yet!
exclaimed the son!

I am too, agreed the father as he playfully tousled his son's hair. *It reminded me of the story of Pharaoh killing all the boy babies when Moses was born.*

And Moses became a shepherd like us!
replied the son.

Father and son sat still for a while just thinking about that wonderful event so many years ago

Suddenly the son jumped up and exclaimed,
We don't even know the baby's name!
If we did, maybe we would've heard about him. Surely he wasn't killed in the slaughter!

No, I don't think God would allow the long-awaited Messiah to be killed, responded the father.

Maybe we didn't hear anything because he was just growing up and God was getting him ready to be the Messiah! added the son.

Perhaps you're right, nodded the father, *since just a few months ago…..*

…we heard about a prophet who was healing people and, not too far from here had raised a man to life who had been dead four days! You remember that!

Yeah. whispered the son. *Cousin Jacob told me. The prophet's name was Jesus and all he did was stand in front of the tomb and call out the man's name and out he came all wrapped up in linen cloth! Weird!*

I wonder about him, pondered the father.
His name, Jesus, means God saves.

But, father, lots of guys have that same name!

That's true. Still…..

Cousin Jacob also told me, added the son,
that that same prophet, Jesus, was crucified a few weeks ago in
Jerusalem. God wouldn't allow that to happen to the Messiah!
And he was hung between two criminals which means he was
the worst!

I heard the same thing, sighed the father.
The governor even had his crime posted on the cross that he
was King of the Jews.

King? like David was king?
exclaimed the son.

That's what I heard.

But I also heard that he came back to life just like the man he himself raised to life!

Who raised him? asked the son.

That's the peculiar thing! They said the tomb was sealed with a large stone, there were soldiers guarding it, and, yet three days after he died, he was alive and walking and talking just like before!

Totally awed, the son shouted *God raised him!*

I think you're right, son.
There's no other explanation. Maybe….
…..Maybe it's time we went to see him. I think he may be the Messiah and the baby I saw long ago.

Jacob can take care of the sheep again, eh father?!!!
slyly winked the son looking at his father.

So off went the father and son in search of the Messiah. They headed in the direction of Jerusalem where they thought he might be.

As they walked, they talked about him and wondered how they would know him if they did see him.

How will we know him if we see him?
asked the son.
You said when you saw him he looked just like any other baby boy.

I don't know, son. Some people had said he called himself The Good Shepherd, so maybe he was shepherding?

I like to picture him like that! mused the son.
I wonder about his flock, though.
Did he take his sheep into Jerusalem?

Prophets often spoke words that had deeper meaning,
replied the father.
If he is the Messiah, he came to save us and we're not sheep! So maybe his flock is people like us.

Then we should be looking for a bunch of people!
cried the son.

This idea spurred them into taking faster steps and taking note of the people they might see,

  especially if there was a lot of people.

When they met some men who were headed to Bethany, they remembered that Jesus had friends in Bethany! That's where he raised the dead man!

So they asked the men if they could keep them company.

As they all walked, the father and son mentioned that they were looking for the prophet, Jesus, since they heard that he was alive after being dead.

The men had heard the same thing, too! And they had seen Jesus before he was crucified and had heard him tell how he was The Good Shepherd! And that his flock is people he came to save!

Turning to his father, the son whispered,

Wow, father! You were right!
Do you think he came to save us, too?
        and then a little louder,
but what's he saving us from?!!

One of the men with them smiled when he heard the son's question and stopped to explain that The Good Shepherd, Jesus, came to redeem us back into God's good grace.

Excitedly the son turned to his father,

That's what you said the angels said on the night he was born!

Then one of the other men cried,
Look! Over on that hill, there's a big crowd.

Let's see what it's all about!

As they raced past olive orchards, they kept looking ahead to see more clearly.

Suddenly they stood still in their tracks – all of them!

They saw a cloud come down from the sky and go up again and disappear – not like any clouds they had ever seen before!

Quickly they ran all the more towards the crowd to see what was happening.

When they arrived, the people in the crowd reminded the father of his family those many years ago when they had seen the angels announce the Messiah's birth.

Everyone was talking at once!

Finally, they asked what had happened.

The man closest to them replied:
We were with Jesus who was telling us that he was leaving but he was sending the Holy Spirit and we would be empowered to be his witnesses throughout the whole earth!

Then, he was lifted up in a cloud and while we were gazing intently into the sky, two men in white clothing stood beside us and spoke!

The son's eyes grew wide as he clutched and squeezed his father's hand remembering his father's story of long ago.

What did they say? he asked.

They said that Jesus was coming back just like he left us!
He's coming back!

Did you hear that, father? Maybe we'll see him next time!

Then the man put his hand on the son's shoulder and explained how the son and father could be sure to see him the next time.

And so began the witnessing.

Not only will the father and son see him next time Jesus comes back, but they will be raised from the dead just like Jesus was. And Jesus will take them to heaven to live with him forever. After all, Jesus is the Lamb of God who takes away the sin of the world. He was the perfect sacrifice even better than the lambs from the father's field.

Jesus will come back for you, too, if you believe with all your heart that He is the Lamb of God who took away your sin.

Endnotes

1 Ps 8:3-4 ESV
2 Luke 2:14 NASB

Printed in the United States
by Baker & Taylor Publisher Services